For Harry, who inspired it. M. W.

For Willie, who found a good friend. B. F.

Library of Congress Cataloging-in-Publication Data.
Waddell, Martin. Hi, Harry! / Martin Waddell ; illustrated by Barbara Firth. —1st U.S. ed. p.   cm.
"The moving story of how one slow tortoise slowly made a friend." Summary: A tortoise tries
to find someone who will play with him at his own speed. ISBN 0-7636-1802-0
[1. Turtles—Fiction. 2. Snails—Fiction. 3. Speed—Fiction.
4. Friendship—Fiction. 5. Animals—Fiction.] I. Firth, Barbara, ill. II. Title.
PZ7.W1137 Hk 2003 [E]—dc21 2001047140 Printed in Italy 10 9 8 7 6 5 4 3 2 1
This book was typeset in Godlike. The illustrations were done in watercolor and ink.
Candlewick Press, 2067 Massachusetts Avenue, Cambridge, Massachusetts 02140
visit us at www.candlewick.com

HI, HARRY!

Martin Waddell

illustrated by

Barbara Firth

CANDLEWICK PRESS
CAMBRIDGE, MASSACHUSETTS

Harry Tortoise
sat on his tree stump.

He wanted
to play . . .

but he had no one
to play with.

Along came Buster Rabbit.

"Hi, Buster!" said Harry.
"Can I play with you?"

"Can't stop. Got to keep going!"
Buster called.

"Going where?"
Harry asked.

But Buster
was gone.

Stan Badger came by.
"Hi, Stan!" said Harry.

"Can't talk now!"
Stan called.

"Why not?"
Harry asked.

But Stan Badger
was gone.

Along came Sarah Mouse.
"Hi, Sarah!" said Harry.

"I've got to hop. Can't be late!" Sarah said.

"Late for what?"
Harry asked.

But Sarah Mouse
wasn't there anymore.

"I wish I had someone to play with," thought Harry.

"Someone not quick who has time to play with a tortoise."

Harry set off . . .

so slow slow

. . . . slowly

to find someone
to play with.

"Hi, Mushroom," said Harry.

"Hi, Rock,"
said Harry.

"Hi, Pond,"
said Harry.

"Hi, Harry,"
said Harry to Harry.

"Hi, Harry!"
said someone.

"Who said that?"
gasped Harry.

"It was me,"
said Sam Snail.
"Can I play with
you, Harry?"

"YES!"
Harry said.

They played Slow Races.

Heads In and . . .

Heads Out.

Turn Around and . . .

Turn Around Again.

Then they sat by the pool and
they talked and talked about
being a tortoise, and being a snail,
about tree stumps and puddles,
and mushrooms and moss,
and the trouble with rabbits
and badgers and mice . . .

and how good
it is to be
slow.

And how nice, how very very very nice, it is to be . . . friends.